# A CHRISTMAS SWEATER FOR NINA

Cecilia Heikkilä

Crocodile Books, USA
An imprint of Interlink Publishing Group, Inc.
www.interlinkbooks.com

Nina the cat's house was right in the middle of the city.
It wasn't very warm in there at this time of year.
The floor was icy and cold air came through the door.

But her sweater was warm and woolly.

Early every morning, Nina took a walk through the small town
to keep warm.

The city was in a festive mood that morning.

The snow had come during the night and each and every animal, small and big, was shopping for Christmas presents or a Christmas tree.

Some were in a hurry, but most of them took time to enjoy a chat with their neighbors and friends.

As Nina passed shop windows, she smelled cinnamon buns from the bakery and she heard the mice singing Christmas carols.

"Excuse me, I think you lost something," said the smallest mouse, but Nina had already walked past and did not hear his quiet voice.

Nina walked farther and farther. But after a while, her belly started to get cold ...

Oh no! The sweater had unraveled and
there was only a long strand of yarn left.
Everything had just gotten worse for
this cat who lived in a cardboard box.

Suddenly the yarn was being pulled away and beginning
a journey of its own. Nina quickly caught the end.
Where was it going? Best to follow it!

The yarn was circling around ...

... through
the mice's choir ...

... and straight over
Esther the raccoon's hat.

It swooshed and swirled over houses and chimneys.

Looped and twisted over
rooftops and towers.

It went through the door, inside the Saffron Buns café ...

... and quickly out again!

Suddenly, it stopped in front of the bookstore. Someone on the other side of the door had been pulling the yarn. A soft humming came from inside.

Nina opened the door carefully ...

It was warm and pleasant inside the bookstore.

Ms. Badger sat in front of the crackling fire. She held something red and woolly in her paws.

"Oh, how nice that you found the rest of the yarn," she said. "Now I can finally finish my knitting project. Would you like to stay for a cup of tea?"

Even though Nina lost her
sweater on that cold winter day,
she found a new home in
Ms. Badger's bookstore.

And if I remember correctly, they still
live there today.